POKÉMON

CAPTURE THE CLAYDOL!

ADAPTED BY
TRACEY WEST

SCHOLASTIC INC.

New York   Toronto   London   Auckland   Sydney
Mexico City   New Delhi   Hong Kong   Buenos Aires

ISBN 0-439-89049-7

Published by Scholastic Inc. SCHOLASTIC and associated logos are trademarks and/or registered trademarks of Scholastic Inc.

12 11 10 9 8   7 8 9 10/0

Designed by Kay Petronio
Printed in the U.S.A.

First printing, December 2006

Ash and his friends walked across Izabe
Island. Then Ash saw something strange on
top of a mountain.

"Look up there, you guys!" Ash called
out. "It's a giant Poké Ball!"

"I can tell you about the stone Poké
Ball," someone said.

Ash turned around. He saw an old man
with a long cape and white beard.

"I am Sigourney, the sage of Izabe
Island," the man said.

Sigourney took out an old book from under his cape. Then he told the story.

"Centuries ago, a great power was sealed inside the Poké Ball," he began. "An evil stranger released the destructive force from the ball. This force destroyed the island!"

"Then a white sage sealed the Destroyer inside another giant Poké Ball," Sigourney said. "That Poké Ball has sat in the middle of Izabe Lake for years."

"Wow!" Ash cried.

"I can prove my story is true," Sigourney said. "I will take you to the lake."

Ash did not know it, but Team Rocket heard the whole story.

"Whatever that power is, we should steal it," James said.

Jessie agreed. "Let's get to the lake before those twerps do!"

Ash and his friends walked to the lake with Sigourney. The giant Poké Ball sat in the middle of the lake.

"No one has touched it for a thousand years," the sage said.

Then Ash saw something in the sky.

"That's Team Rocket's balloon!" Ash yelled.

Jessie grinned. "Let's pop open that rock and see what our prize is!"

Meowth pressed a button on a remote control. The bottom of the balloon opened up.

Bam! Bam! Bam! A bunch of bombs dropped on the rock.

The giant Poké Ball shattered. It glowed with bright light.

A huge creature burst from the Poké Ball!

"I think it's a Claydol," Brock said.

"A really big Claydol!" Ash pointed out. "The horrible Destroyer from the story was really a giant Pokémon?"

Team Rocket tried to pick up the giant
Claydol.

"*Claydol,*" the Pokémon boomed.

Claydol hit the balloon with two freezing
blasts from its arms. Then it blasted the
balloon with fire.

"We're blasting off again!" Team Rocket cried.

They fell from the sky . . . and landed on top of Claydol's head!

Claydol slowly flew across the lake.

"Do you think it will attack the village?" May asked.

Claydol flew to the woods. It shot flames from its arms. The fire burned a path through the trees.

"I guess that answers your question," Brock said.

"It is big, but a Pokémon is still a Pokémon," Ash said. "I will catch it with a Poké Ball!"

Ash threw a Poké Ball at the giant Claydol. It opened up, and a red light came out. But the light faded quickly.

"No good!" Max said. "I guess an ordinary Poké Ball is not enough for a Claydol that big."

"We will have to use the stone ball on top of the mountain," Sigourney said.

"How will we get it up there?" May asked.

Sigourney looked through the old book. "It says a beautiful maiden made the Claydol using mud from the lake, so the white sage used Water techniques against it."

Brock threw out two Poké Balls.

"Mudkip! Lombre! Come on out!" he called.

The two Water Pokémon blasted the big Claydol with streams of water. Claydol blasted the streams back at them. The water soaked everyone!

"I guess I read the book wrong," Sigourney said.

Team Rocket fell off of Claydol's head.
They landed in front of Ash and his friends.
   "Let us help you catch that Claydol,"
James said.
   Ash wasn't sure if he wanted help from
bad guys. But Claydol was so big . . .
   "I guess we could use some help," Ash said.

Sigourney looked in the book for another way to catch the Claydol.

"Aha! This chapter may have the answer," the sage said. "Claydol is hungry. We can use food as bait. The book says Claydol loves eggplant."

A big Claydol needs a big eggplant. So
Ash and James dressed up like the purple
plant. They danced around.

"Claydol, over here!" James called out.

"We're delicious!" Ash yelled.

Claydol followed the boys. But it did not look hungry. It looked angry!

"What is this?" Sigourney said. "I read the book wrong again. It says Claydol hates eggplant!"

Claydol chased Ash and James to a dead end. It stared at them with angry eyes. Then it began to stomp up and down.

"Take off your costumes before it hurts you!" May yelled. The boys took off their costumes just in time.

Slam! Claydol crushed the costumes.

"Does the book say anything else?" May asked Sigourney.

"Yes," said the sage. "The giant Claydol went to the village to find the beautiful maiden who created it. The white sage dressed up like a maiden to lead the Claydol away from town."

May, Jessie, Meowth, and Wobbuffet
dressed up.

"I don't know why you three are out
here," Jessie said. "I am the only beautiful
maiden on this mountain!"

"Maidens are supposed to be young, sweet, and nice," May said. "Not bad guys!"

"How dare you say I am not young and sweet!" Jessie said.

Claydol heard the maidens talking. It flew over.

Bam! Claydol blasted Jessie with fire.
Bam! Claydol blasted Meowth with ice.
Bam! Claydol blasted May with air.
But Claydol did not blast Wobbuffet.
Claydol thought Wobbuffet was beautiful.

Wobbuffet ran to the mountain. Claydol chased it.

"Release the giant Poké Ball!" Brock yelled.

Ash and the others used a lever to get the Poké Ball loose. It rolled down the mountain.

The giant Poké Ball got stuck on a ridge.
"We've got to hurry!" Max warned.

Brock called on Mudkip and Lombre. They
blasted the Poké Ball with water. It came
loose. Then Pikachu hit it with Thunder.

Bam! The Poké Ball sped down the hill . . .

Slam! The Poké Ball hit Claydol. The ball trapped the giant Pokémon.

"We did it!" Ash cried.

"And it's all thanks to Wobbuffet," Brock said.

"Hey, where did Team Rocket go?" May asked.

The Team Rocket balloon flew up above. Team Rocket caught the Poké Ball in a big rope.

"Claydol is ours!" Jessie cried.

But the giant Poké Ball kept rolling down the mountain.

The rope wrapped around and around the ball.

The rope broke—and sent Team Rocket's balloon flying over the hills.

"Team Rocket's blasting off again!" they screamed.

The Poké Ball kept rolling. It landed in the lake.

"Claydol is right back where it started," May said.

"I hope no one ever sets it free again," Brock said.

Ash thought about the powerful blasts of the giant Claydol.

"I hope so, too!" he agreed.